The Case of the
Phantom Cat

For Lucy, Sinead, Madeleine, and Tabitha,
who told me how much they loved Maisie!
—H.W.

For Sylvie and Graham, with all my love
—M.L.

Text copyright © 2013 by Holly Webb
Illustrations copyright © 2013 Marion Lindsay
First published in Great Britain in 2013 by Stripes Publishing,
an imprint of Little Tiger Press.

www.hmhco.com

Text set in Adobe Garamond

The Library of Congress has cataloged the hardcover edition as follows:
Webb, Holly.
The case of the phantom cat/written by Holly Webb;
illustrated by Marion Lindsay.
p. cm.—(The mysteries of Maisie Hitchens)
Summary: Alice's father invites twelve-year-old Maisie and her dog Eddie to
join Alice on a trip to the country, but the manor her father has rented seems
to be haunted, terrifying Alice and putting Maisie's detecting skills to the test.
Includes quizzes, activities, and more.
[1. Mystery and detective stories—Fiction. 2. Haunted houses—Fiction.
3. Cats—Fiction. 4. Great Britain—History—Victoria, 1837–1901—Fiction.]
I. Lindsay, Marion, illustrator. II. Title.
PZ7.W367Cam 2015
[Fic]—dc23
2014044669

ISBN: 978-0-544-58243-9 hardcover
ISBN: 978-0-544-81084-6 paperback

Manufactured in the United States of America
DOC 10 9 8 7 6 5 4 3 2 1
4500608319

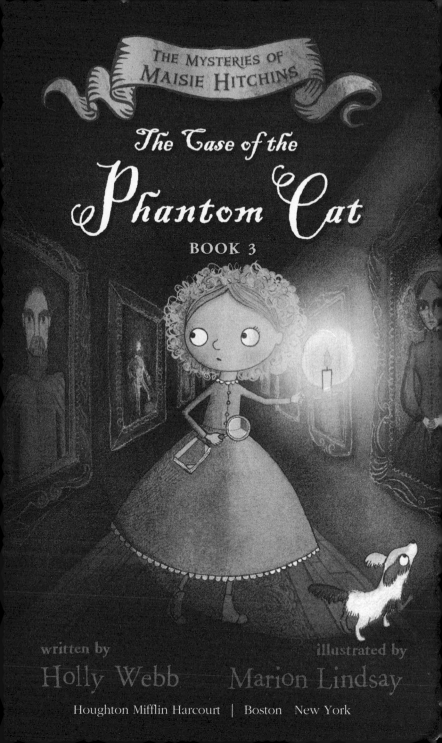

THE MYSTERIES OF
MAISIE HITCHINS

The Case of the
Phantom Cat

BOOK 3

written by

Holly Webb

illustrated by

Marion Lindsay

Houghton Mifflin Harcourt | Boston New York

31 Albion Street, London

Attic:

Maisie's grandmother and Sally the maid

Third floor:

Miss Lane's rooms

Second floor:

Madame Lorimer's rooms

First floor:

Professor Tobin's rooms

Ground floor:

Entrance hall, sitting room, and dining room

Basement:

Maisie's room, kitchen, and yard entrance

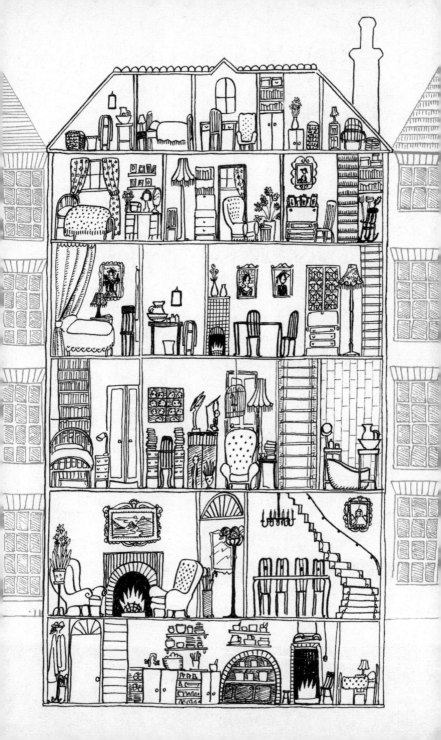

Maisie dusted the Chinese vase on the hall table again. It wasn't the slightest bit grubby anymore, but she wanted an excuse to hang around abovestairs and she'd polished everything else she could find. She was waiting for her friend Alice to come for her French conversation lesson with Madame Lorimer, who lodged on the second floor. The hall clock struck the quarter hour, and

Maisie sighed. Alice clearly wasn't coming. Again. She had missed her lesson for the third week in a row now.

Maisie picked up her dusters and the beeswax polish and walked slowly down the back stairs to the kitchen, where Sally, the maid, was peeling potatoes at the big table. Maisie's grandmother was poking at a saucepan on the range, boiling a treacle sponge pudding for the lodgers' dinner.

The house at 31 Albion Street was divided up into apartments on the different floors and rented out to lodgers. The best rooms on the first floor were rented to Professor Tobin, who had filled them with glass cases full of strange stuffed animals and other odd relics that he had collected on his travels. An actress, Miss Lottie Lane, lived on the third floor, and of course Madame

Lorimer, the French teacher, was on the second.

"Goodness, have you only just finished?" Gran frowned at Maisie.

Maisie crouched down to fuss over Eddie, her dog. He had been asleep in his basket close to the stove, but now he was leaping up at her happily, his ears flapping. "Oh . . . Were you waiting for Miss Alice again?" Gran said.

"She must be very ill," Maisie murmured worriedly as she stroked Eddie's silky ears. "It's more than a fortnight now since we've seen her."

"They sent a message to Madame Lorimer, though, didn't they?" Gran asked, putting the lid back on the pan and dabbing her steam-reddened face with her apron. "Did they not say what was wrong?"

"A putrid sore throat—that was all her governess said." Maisie glanced anxiously at Gran. "But it might have got worse. What if Alice has scarlet fever? George told me that a little girl who lives on his street has it and she's very bad. The fever's spread all through the school."

George, the butcher's boy, had been gorily dramatic about the scarlet fever when he'd delivered the meat that morning. He'd told Maisie that Elizabeth, the little girl who lived a few houses down from his family, was bright red and bumpy all over. He said she looked like a strawberry. Although, come to think of it, how did George know? He'd hardly have gone visiting. But at the time she'd been so fascinated by his description of Elizabeth the strawberry that she hadn't thought to ask.

"And then her skin all started peeling off!" George had hissed.

It was like some dreadful ghost story, Maisie thought. "Is it catching?" she'd asked him.

"Catching! Of course it's catching!"
George rolled his eyes at her. "Half the
school's got it. And there's nothing you can
do, you know." He shrugged. "Some people
get better. But most don't," he added, biting
his lip. "I just hope my little sister's going
to be all right. She was playing hopscotch
in the street with Elizabeth just a few days
ago. I don't want her going down with the
scarlatina."

Maisie frowned. "Scarlatina?" It sounded
like some particularly nasty sort of fairy.
Perhaps one that went around making
people ill. Turning them into strawberries
with one flick of her wand.

"Same thing," George explained gloomily.
"Just another name for it. Oh, well. Better get
on."

Now Maisie looked wide-eyed at Gran,

imagining Alice with an awful scarlet rash.

Gran sniffed. "But Miss Alice doesn't go to school, does she? She has her own governess. So she would hardly have been mixing with those sorts of children. And she's too old for scarlet fever, surely. Don't fuss, Maisie. The poor child probably just has a sore throat, like that governess of hers said."

Maisie smiled. "If Alice has any sense, she'll stay ill for as long as she can. I'd be ill if I had to have lessons from a governess as horrible as Miss Sidebotham every day." But she was still playing with Eddie's ears, running them through her fingers and furrowing her brow. "Do you think I could go and visit her?"

"Did you dust everywhere upstairs?" Gran asked.

"Yes," Maisie sighed. She didn't enjoy

housework, but she was good at it because she'd had a great deal of practice. Even though they owned their house and it was a tall one on a smart-ish London street, they certainly weren't rich, and Gran needed Maisie's help.

Thirty-one Albion Street had a great many stairs, and there was a lot of it to keep clean. Between Maisie and Gran and Sally, they managed it all and made a respectable living from the lodgers. But it had meant that Maisie had had to leave school well before she was twelve to help. Gran had told her that if anyone asked, she was to say that she had lessons from Madame Lorimer. There had been seventy children in Maisie's class at school, though, and Maisie reckoned her teacher had hardly noticed she was gone.

"Oh, go on then, Maisie. Go and see Miss Alice and find out how she is!"

"Can I really?" Maisie hugged her. "Oh, but, Gran, they won't let me in to visit her looking like this, will they?" Maisie looked down at her faded wool dress and her apron. She was clean and neat, but certainly not smart. The servants at Alice's lovely house would know at once that she wasn't a suitable friend for a young lady.

"Go to the kitchen door, Maisie, for goodness' sake. All this detecting and you still haven't an ounce of common sense. Ask after Miss Alice and say Madame Lorimer sent you. Tell them you've a message for her, sending her good wishes, or something like that. And put your hat on!" Gran called as Maisie dashed out of the kitchen. "Oh, and don't forget the dog! He's getting under my feet!"

Maisie tiptoed down the steps into the basement and knocked quietly at the kitchen door of Alice's house. She had never been inside before—they usually met at Maisie's or occasionally in the street when Alice was out walking. But she was almost always with a maid or her governess, which meant they couldn't do much more than smile and wave. Maisie had seen Miss Sidebotham tell Alice off for even that.

"Now be good," she whispered to Eddie sternly. He had seen a cat on their way over and Maisie hadn't managed to grab his collar in time. He had barked madly and chased it halfway down the street, nearly tripping up several ladies out shopping. It had taken her ages to catch him, and it was very embarrassing.

Eddie looked up at her innocently and

wagged his tail. Maisie sighed. He clearly didn't feel guilty in the slightest.

Maisie was about to knock again when the kitchen maid answered the door. "Whatever do you want?" She stared at Maisie in surprise, then eyed Eddie suspiciously.

Maisie smiled at her, trying not to look nervous. "I've come to bring a message for Miss Alice Lacey," she explained. "From Madame Lorimer, her French teacher. Madame wants to know how Miss Alice is."

"Oh . . ." The girl, who wasn't all that much older than Maisie, nodded. "I suppose you'd better come in then . . . Not him!" she added, in a genteel shriek, pointing at Eddie. "Cook would have my guts for garters. You'd better tie him up outside."

"I'll be back soon, I promise," Maisie whispered to Eddie as she twisted the rope through the railings. "I should have put your diamond collar on—that would show her." Maisie and Eddie had tracked down an emerald and pearl necklace for a young actress, and the actress's fiancé, who was a lord, had sent both Maisie and Eddie jewels

12

as a reward. Maisie was very proud of her bracelet and Eddie's collar, but they were a bit of a worry to wear. She kept them hanging on the wall of her room instead, in a little glass case that Professor Tobin had given her.

"Who is it, Lizzie?" someone called, and the maid bustled Maisie in.

"She's come calling for Miss Alice. From her French teacher," the maid said, pushing Maisie ahead of her, so that she ended up standing in front of a large newspaper. Its reader was sitting at a scrubbed wooden table much like Gran's, except that it was in the middle of a kitchen about four times the size, with the very newest, smartest, shiniest kitchen range and shelves of huge tins and trays and china.

The person reached around her paper for the cup of tea that was next to her on the table, and then folded the paper up so she could stare at Maisie. It was the cook. "Would you be the young lady that Miss Alice mentioned?" she asked. "Been working at a theater? Hunting for lost jewelry?"

"Yes." Maisie nodded, hoping that this wasn't going to get her thrown out. If the cook knew about the mysterious missing emerald, it could only be because Alice had told her. Perhaps she and Alice were friends. "Is Miss Alice any better?" she asked anxiously. "We only heard that she had a bad sore throat, but I haven't seen her for weeks."

The cook took a sip from her teacup. "She's been confined to her room. They did think it might be diphtheria, but that was just the ninny of a governess making a fuss. Any news from upstairs this afternoon, Lizzie?" she said to the kitchen maid.

"Miss Alice said could she not have milk pudding for her supper again, but Miss Sidebotham said it was that or calves'-foot jelly. So the upstairs maids told me, anyway. And after Miss Sidebotham had gone, Miss

Alice told Mary-Ann that if she brought her calves'-foot jelly, she'd throw it in the fire."

Maisie giggled. "She sounds as though she's getting better, then."

The cook nodded at her approvingly. "Did I hear Lizzie telling you to tie up a dog?"

"I did tie him up very carefully," Maisie promised. But she checked behind her just in case Eddie had slipped his collar and followed her.

"I'm sure you did, dear. But Miss Alice likes dogs. I always used to let her cut them out of gingerbread. Dogs and elephants. And I haven't an elephant on hand to cheer her up, so I reckon you and a dog might do. Lizzie, fetch me some of that gingerbread you made yesterday."

"But Miss Alice is only having milk pudding!" Lizzie protested.

"Stuff and nonsense. She'll waste away, poor child. Go and fetch your dog, Miss Whatever-Your-Name-Is. Then you can leave your cape and hat here. And, Lizzie, find Mary-Ann. You can't go sneaking upstairs."

When Maisie came back in with Eddie, who was wagging his tail madly at the delicious smells coming out of the range, there was another maid in the kitchen, wearing a smart black dress, a frilled apron, and a pretty cap. But despite her nice outfit, she beamed at Maisie in a friendly sort of way and cooed over Eddie.

"Little sweetheart! He's bound to make Miss Alice feel better. Come on—I've found a laundry basket. Will he jump in it, if Miss Sidebotham comes spying around?"

Maisie nodded. "He'll stay if I tell him." Which was *almost* always true.

Mary-Ann hurried Maisie up the back stairs. "These go all the way to the first floor," she explained, puffing as she lugged the big wicker basket along. "There's a flight of marble stairs down to the main hall, but we don't use that. Shhh!" They were in a beautifully carpeted passage now and Maisie could hear someone coming—someone with slow, heavy footsteps.

"The butler!" Mary-Ann whispered. "He's a real stickler, likes everything perfect. Put the little dog in the basket!"

Mary-Ann whipped the plate of gingerbread out of the basket where she'd been carrying it balanced on top of the washing, and Maisie dropped Eddie in and covered him in a sheet. Eddie poked his nose out and peered at her, his ears twitching doubtfully, but when she put her finger to her lips and shushed him, he wriggled back underneath.

Just in time, Mary-Ann pushed Maisie behind a long velvet curtain. Maisie held her breath as the footsteps rounded the corner of the passage and came to a stop.

"What are you doing, girl?" a treacly voice inquired.

"Miss Sidebotham said she thought Miss Alice's pillowcases should be changed, sir. What with her having a temperature . . ."

"Hmm. Don't let the master of the house see you carrying baskets of washing about," he said.

"No, sir." Maisie could tell that Mary-Ann was trying not to giggle. She hoped it wasn't because the washing was wriggling too much.

"He's gone!" Mary-Ann whispered finally from around the curtain. "Come on! Hurry!"

Maisie grabbed Eddie out of the basket and followed the older girl down the hallway. They were going too quickly for her to take in much of the house, except that it seemed to sparkle. All the curtains were made of the same rich velvet as the one she'd been hiding behind, and pictures glittered at her from gilded frames.

"This is Miss Alice's room." Mary-Ann knocked lightly and opened the door, holding it for Maisie and Eddie to walk in.

Maisie couldn't help gasping at the prettiness of Alice's room. The bed was draped with flowered curtains and there were two pink velvet chairs on either side of the fire. At one side of the room was the most enormous dollhouse, so big that it needed a table all to itself.

"Maisie!" Alice had been lying down, just a small lump under the lace-covered bedspread, but she sat up, staring. She looked dreadful, Maisie thought, examining her anxiously. Her face was a pale yellow, with dark shadows around her eyes, and her pretty blond hair had gone all stringy. But at least she wasn't in the slightest bit strawberry-looking.

"Now don't excite yourself, miss!" Mary-Ann whispered. "Cook sent her up here, but we don't want you taking a turn for the worse. I'll stay outside and pretend to be dusting—then I can let you know if anyone comes. And Cook's sent you up some gingerbread, miss." Mary-Ann took it out of the basket again and laid it on a little table, then whisked out to guard the door.

"What happens if someone does come?"
Alice asked, wide-eyed. Her voice was croaky,
as though her throat still wasn't quite better.

"I'll hide under the bed," Maisie said.
She checked beneath the frilly dust ruffle. "I
could practically live under here!" Then she
perched by Alice's feet and looked at her
worriedly. "You don't look well. I did wonder
whether you might have scarlet fever."

Alice shook her head. "No. Miss Sidebotham says it was all because I went for a walk when it was raining and didn't bother to change my stockings afterward, but I think that's nonsense." She sighed. "I'm ever so sick of being ill. It's boring. It's so nice that you and Eddie have come."

"Haven't you had other visitors?" Maisie asked as she put Eddie down on the bed.

"No—people probably thought it was scarlet fever and didn't want to risk it. But Papa visits me every day when he gets back from his office. He said he was going to have a surprise for me today—something I should really like. I tried to guess, but he wouldn't tell." Alice smiled at Maisie. "There you are, a chance to practice your detecting. You can tell me what the surprise is. Solve the mystery for me!"

Maisie pulled her magnifying glass out of her coat pocket and laid it on the silken bedcover. Then she found her notebook and pencil stub and stared at Alice, trying to put on a serious detective face. "Any clues?"

"No-ooo . . ." Alice shook her head. "He said I was sure to like it, that's all." She reached over to stroke Eddie. "Perhaps he's bought me a dog! Or a kitten . . ." She gave a little sigh. "Sorry, Eddie. But I would love a kitten. Oh, I hope Papa won't be held up at the office." She peered at the little gilt clock on the mantelpiece. "He should be here any minute, I think."

Maisie squeaked and jumped off the bed. "I'd better go then!"

Alice laughed. "Oh, don't! He'd like you."

The door suddenly flew open and Mary-Ann peered around the edge of it, flapping her hands at Maisie. "It's Mr. Lacey! Hide!"

Maisie looked at the frilly dust ruffle around the bed, but Alice caught her hand. "Honestly. I've told him all about your adventures, Maisie. He won't be cross."

Footsteps sounded and a tall, fair-haired man strode in and stopped in surprise when he saw Maisie and Eddie.

"Papa!" Alice called out croakily. "This is Maisie—the girl I told you about! She came to visit because I'd not been to my French lesson for so long and she was worried."

"That's very good of you." Mr. Lacey gave Maisie a little half bow. She bobbed her knees in a curtsey and started to sidle toward the door.

"Don't go, Maisie!" Alice pleaded.

Maisie looked across at Mr. Lacey, who nodded, waving her toward one of the pink velvet chairs.

"Alice is right—please do stay. I haven't seen her looking this bright for a fortnight. She's even got color in her cheeks." He smiled at her. "And I've some very good news for you, dearest Alice." Alice's father tugged thoughtfully at the end of his blond mustache.

Maisie watched him, wondering what it was he did at his office to make so much money. This was the largest, grandest house she had ever been in. It was even grander than the theater she'd worked at, which had been quite shabby when you saw it without the gaslights and the excitement of the show.

It was difficult to detect someone who was sitting next to you, Maisie realized. She couldn't stare at Mr. Lacey without being rude. She had to make do with quick glances. She thought he must smoke cigars, or perhaps a pipe—his mustache was stained brown at the ends. And his front teeth stuck out a little! A pipe, then, and he'd held it in his teeth so much that it had pushed them out. Maisie felt quite proud of herself.

"So, shall I tell you about my surprise?"

Mr. Lacey asked, interrupting Maisie's thoughts.

"Oh, yes, please! I've been wondering all day." Alice sat up further against her lace-edged pillows, watching him eagerly.

Her father beamed at her. "I've rented a house in the country for you to go to, my dear, so that you can breathe the fresh air and get properly well."

Alice's eyes widened. "Are you coming too?" she asked hopefully.

"I wish I could," her father told her. "But I have to be at the office. Miss Sidebotham will go with you."

"Oh . . ." Alice sighed and drooped against her pillows.

Her father watched her anxiously and tugged his mustache again. "Unless . . . Unless you would like to go too, Miss Maisie?"

Chapter Two

Maisie stared at him blankly. Even with all her careful detecting, she'd certainly never expected him to say that. "Me?" she gasped.

"Oh, yes, yes, what a simply perfect plan!" Alice croaked. "Oh, Maisie, please say that you will."

"I'd have to ask Gran," Maisie murmured, but she was smiling hopefully to herself. She had never been out of London—it would be an amazing adventure to travel to the country.

She could see why Mr. Lacey wanted Alice to go. London this winter had been full of thick, choking fog. Sometimes it had been so bad that it was dark even at midday, and if Maisie went out in it, the fog seemed to seep into her lungs so that she could taste it for the rest of the day. It seeped into the houses, too, under the doors and through the cracks in the windows, so it was impossible to escape. The thought of somewhere with trees and grass, which Maisie had only seen in the public parks, was wonderful.

Mr. Lacey nodded. "Indeed, you must ask your grandmother." He patted Eddie's head, smiling. "And, of course, you'll take the little dog, too. You two would be the best sort of medicine for my dear girl, I should think. When Alice is feeling stronger, you could go out for walks with this little chap. Can you wait a little longer, Maisie? I will write a letter for you to take back to your grandmother now, with a proper invitation. And I shall promise that Miss Sidebotham will take the very best care of you."

Maisie rolled her eyes at Alice while Mr. Lacey wasn't looking, and Alice had to stuff the frilled sleeve of her nightgown into her mouth to stop herself from laughing.

"If I come, I can help you stay out of her way," Maisie whispered.

Alice nodded hopefully. "It would be such fun!" she whispered back, and she put out her thin little hand and held Maisie's tightly.

"But you've only just come back from that theater!" Gran said, looking from the letter to Maisie and back again. "You're getting rather too much in demand, if you ask me." But she was smiling, so Maisie knew that she was joking.

Maisie sighed. "Don't worry, I'll tell them that I can't go. I can't leave you and Sally to do all the work again. Mr. Lacey said that he had rented the house for a month."

Gran eyed her worriedly. "Having said that, there's ever such a lot of sickness about . . . You're rather old to catch scarlet fever, but even so, I wouldn't put it past you to come down with it, Maisie. And this fog isn't good for anyone. It would do you good to have a few weeks in the country too."

"But how will you manage?" Maisie frowned at her.

Gran sniffed. "Well, there'll be a good deal less scrubbing of floors without that dog tracking mud all over them. He is invited too, isn't he?" she added hopefully.

Maisie nodded. "Alice's father said that once she was a little better, we could take him out for country walks!"

Gran nodded. "And there's still some of the money left from your job at the theater. If I have to, I can get someone in to help."

"So . . . yes?" Maisie held her breath.

"Yes. If you promise me you won't get yourself mixed up in any more mysteries," Gran said. "Just try to behave like a young lady. Like that nice Miss Alice."

"Alice Honoria Lacey! Sit down this instant!" Miss Sidebotham said, in a sort of strangled shriek. She was far too concerned about manners to actually shout across the platform of Paddington Station, but Maisie could tell that she wanted to. Maisie sighed. They had only meant to walk down the platform to get a closer look at the engine, as she had never been on a train before.

Miss Sidebotham was clearly still furious about being saddled with Maisie as well as Alice. And she had been horrified that they were taking Eddie with them—so horrified that she kept on pretending that she just couldn't see him. Maisie could tell Eddie knew that the governess didn't like him. He kept sitting down next to her and giving her long, soulful looks, and then she would trip over him. Maisie couldn't work out if he was trying to win her over or if he was just being annoying.

Miss Sidebotham had protested to Mr. Lacey about them coming, or so Alice had told Maisie. Alice had overheard them talking about it. But her father had told Miss Sidebotham that he felt Alice needed another child with her for more interesting company. He said it was important that she was kept amused while she was recovering. Which obviously meant that he thought Miss Sidebotham was boring as well.

"Which is a great relief to me, Maisie," Alice had told her seriously as they'd waited on the steps of the Laceys' grand house for the cab to take them to the station. "Because Papa is a widower, of course, and one does hear of governesses marrying the master of the house really quite often. Imagine having Miss Sidebotham as a mother!"

"I don't want to," Maisie had said, shuddering.

"Exactly. But if he thinks she's a deathly bore as well, then he can't possibly want to marry her."

"He would be mad!" Maisie told Alice reassuringly, watching Miss Sidebotham snapping at the maids as they carried down the luggage. Her own things were in a rather embarrassingly small and battered leather suitcase that Gran had found in the attic. She could see it now in the pile of cases and boxes waiting to be put in the luggage van, next to Alice's dressing case with her initials embossed in gilt. She did hope that the house they were going to stay in wasn't too grand. Miss Sidebotham was already giving her snooty looks all the time. It would be horrible if the maids at Wisteria Lodge despised her because she didn't have six changes of clothes a day and handmade lace on all of her petticoats.

"Is Wisteria Lodge very big?" she asked Alice as Miss Sidebotham shooed them back across the platform to sit down.

"Quite big," Alice said thoughtfully. "Papa showed me a drawing of it that the house agent sent. It used to be a hunting lodge that belonged to the Marquis of Walden, but he only stayed there for a few weeks every year. And then it was sold. It gets rented out to people who want a country house to stay in. Like us."

Maisie nodded. "What does Wisteria

mean? Is it the name of the village near the house?"

Miss Sidebotham let out a genteel little snort and Maisie went pink.

"I had to ask Papa what it was," Alice said, glaring at her governess. "It's a climbing plant. Very pretty, he said—it has purple flowers. Wisteria Lodge is covered in it in the summer, but we'll only see the bare branches now, of course. The village is called Little Stoney, and that's where the station is."

Maisie looked up at the huge clock hanging above her. "I think the train is due to leave in a few minutes. Look at those great clouds of steam. It's almost as foggy in here as it is out there! Do you think we'd better get on board?"

There were at least eight great engines snorting and bellowing out steam and the occasional spark. Maisie was glad that she had Alice with her—and Eddie, although *he* wasn't much comfort. He didn't like the steam engines either, and he kept having to bark at everything to make himself feel better. A well-bred and snobbish spaniel was also waiting to get aboard the train, and it was giving him the most despising looks.

"Come along, Alice. And you," Miss Sidebotham added with a sigh, as though she would quite like to leave Maisie on the platform. "They've loaded our baggage now, so we must find the compartment your father reserved." She hurried them down the platform into a first-class carriage.

Maisie could hear her muttering that the mongrel should surely be traveling in the guard's van. She picked Eddie up, determined not to let anyone take him away from her.

"Don't let him on the seats!" Miss Sidebotham snapped as Eddie went sniffing around the compartment.

"He wouldn't!" Maisie protested. "He knows he's not allowed on furniture."

"He's a very well-behaved little dog," Alice added. It was unfortunate that the spaniel trotted along the corridor just then and Eddie barked so loudly that the spaniel's grand lady owner asked her maid for smelling salts.

"We should not have brought that . . . creature!" Miss Sidebotham hissed. "He is not fit for polite society."

"He'll be good, miss, I promise," Maisie said breathlessly, catching Eddie and trying to persuade him to curl up nicely under the seat. "I brought him a bone and a blanket to sleep on. He'll be quiet." She rummaged around in the basket Gran had given her for odds and ends, and pulled out the bone — George, her friend from the butcher's shop, had given it to her and it was almost as big as Eddie himself. She reckoned it would last for most of the journey.

The governess collapsed on to the opposite seat with her handkerchief pressed over her face, which Maisie thought was just rude. The bone hardly smelled at all.

"Little Stoney! Little Stoney!" The station-master was striding up and down the platform with his flag, roaring like a foghorn.

"Do hurry, girls! Have you got all your things, Alice? The traveling chess set? Your *Latin Grammar?*"

"Yes, Miss Sidebotham. We really should get off the train now, Miss Sidebotham—the stationmaster is looking most impatient."

The girls tumbled off the train with Eddie dancing excitedly around them. Maisie looked around at the tiny village station. She hadn't really known what to expect—it wasn't a bit like the huge London terminus. Just one short platform, a little ticket office, and a cottage that had to belong to the stationmaster. Miss Sidebotham stood on the platform, counting all the cases. A young boy came over to take them out into the road to be loaded onto a wagon, and she fussed around him.

"We're just going to stretch our legs," Alice called, pulling Maisie and Eddie after her out to the road and ignoring Miss Sidebotham's worried squeaks.

They stood watching the boy handing the cases up onto the wagon, and Maisie noticed gladly that her suitcase really was there. She wouldn't have put it past Miss Sidebotham to leave it behind on purpose.

"So you're the young ladies going to Wisteria Lodge, then?" the boy asked curiously.

Alice went pink and Maisie nodded. "Yes. Is it far from here?"

"No, only a mile or so. But rather you than me."

"What do you mean?" Maisie asked, frowning. "Isn't it a nice house?"

He shrugged. "It's big. But I wouldn't call it nice. It's haunted, for a start."

"Haunted?" Alice gasped and grabbed Maisie's arm.

Maisie snorted. "No, it isn't," she said. "You're just trying to scare us. You don't actually believe in ghosts, do you?"

The boy stopped loading cases and folded his arms, gazing at Maisie and Alice. "The last two—no, three families that took the house have stayed less than a year. Less than a month, the last lot. Strange noises. Odd white shapes in the passageways. The last family went to the vicar and asked him if Wisteria Lodge had been built over a plague pit!"

"What's a plague pit?" Alice whispered. She'd gone horribly white again, so Maisie slipped an arm around her.

"It's a grave for people who died of the plague," Maisie explained. "But I'm sure the house isn't built anywhere near one. Who'd build a house on top of something like that? I bet the vicar told them that. Didn't he?"

"Yes . . ." the boy admitted. "He said it was stuff and nonsense. But they still left!" he added triumphantly. "They said the ghosts definitely smelled like a plague pit!"

"What on earth are you girls doing?" Miss Sidebotham appeared behind them, looking down her nose at the boy. Somehow she managed to make it obvious that she thought it was all Maisie's fault they had fallen into bad company.

"Oh, Miss Sidebotham, this boy says Wisteria Lodge is haunted!" Alice told her in a trembly voice.

"What nonsense," the governess said, but she sounded almost as trembly as Alice.

Maisie rolled her eyes at the boy, who was smirking, obviously very pleased with the success of his story. She squeezed Alice's hand and tried to sound confident. "What a lot of hogwash—there isn't any such thing as ghosts!"

Chapter Three

"It *looks* haunted . . ." Alice said faintly as
the hired carriage drew up outside Wisteria
Lodge.

Maisie peered out the window. The
house didn't look haunted to her. Scarily
large and grand, but that was all. It did have
a rather neglected air, though—there were
a few weeds growing in the drive, and the

windows could have done with a good cleaning.

A smartly dressed maid opened the door, and Maisie could see a huge chandelier hanging in the entrance hall. She was far more worried about forgetting her manners in such a huge place than she was about any ghosts.

"There really isn't any such thing as ghosts," she said comfortingly to Alice. "That boy was just trying to scare us. Boys do that. George does it to me all the time."

"Who is George?" Miss Sidebotham demanded in a shocked voice.

"The butcher's boy, miss," Maisie replied.

"Humph." Miss Sidebotham got down from the carriage and looked over at the house. "Well, it will do, I suppose. I am Miss Sidebotham, Miss Lacey's governess," she said to the maid, her nose in the air as she pranced up the marble steps. "Our luggage is following. We will wait in the drawing room, where we shall require tea." She marched off down the hall, opening doors as she went.

The maid looked surprised and slightly annoyed by the governess's hoity-toity manner, but she smiled at Maisie and Alice as they got down from the carriage.

"Hello!" Maisie smiled back. "This is Miss Alice and I'm Maisie. I've come to keep her company."

"And I'm Annie, miss," the maid told her. "The parlor maid. So you're the poor dear who's been ill?" she said sympathetically to Alice. "Mrs. James—that's the cook—she's planned some lovely meals to fatten you up again, Miss Alice."

Alice beamed at her. "That sounds wonderful. At home they kept trying to make me eat calves'-foot jelly, and I hate it."

"Have you worked here for a long time?" Maisie asked curiously as the maid led them into the house and shut the huge front door. The entrance hall made Maisie feel shabby—the marble staircase shone, even on such a gray day, and the chandelier glittered. There were delicate chairs dotted about—chairs that looked too fragile even for Alice to sit on—and dark, ancient-looking paintings. "Did you work for the marquis who used to own the house?" She was wondering if Annie knew about the ghost stories.

"Goodness no, miss. It's been empty for

ages, this house. Me and Mrs. James and Cissie and Lily, the other maids, we've all just come up from the village, only a couple of days before you. We've been up all hours, trying to get the old place ready. It's meant a lot of work, since the house has been empty so long. Some of the rooms are still under dust sheets, but Mr. Lawrence, the house agent, he said you might not need them all, being as there's only the three of you."

Alice giggled. "How many bedrooms are there?"

"I lost count, miss," Annie told her. "We've got the nicest ones ready, though. Must be at least fifteen of them altogether, I'd say."

Maisie looked at Alice. "Ooh, I don't know. I think I need at least fifteen bedrooms."

"And a couple of parlors and a breakfast room," Alice added firmly.

"We're teasing," Maisie told Annie hurriedly when she saw a worried expression flit across her face.

"We made the lilac parlor ready for you, miss, and the drawing room and the dining room, but the breakfast room's still all shut up . . ."

"You must have worked terribly hard," Alice said seriously. "We are grateful."

"Even if Miss Sidebotham looks like a mouse died under her nose," Maisie added. "Don't worry. She's always like that." She eyed Annie sideways. "The boy loading the luggage said that the last people here didn't stay very long. Did you work for them, too?"

Annie shook her head. "No, in the past people have always brought their own servants with them."

"Oh . . ." Maisie hesitated, but Alice elbowed her in the ribs.

"Ask her!"

"The boy said Wisteria Lodge was haunted . . ." Maisie said. "Is it?" She crossed her fingers under her jacket. She didn't want Alice even more worried. "It must be just a story, surely."

Annie looked around to see if anyone else was listening—perhaps she thought Miss Sidebotham would disapprove of her gossiping with the girls, which was almost certainly true. Maisie glanced over her shoulder to make sure the governess was still safely in the drawing room.

"The last two lots of lodgers certainly did leave in a tearing hurry, miss! Last time it was a lady and a gentleman, and they left in the middle of the night—their carriage went galloping through the village as though the hounds of hell was after them!"

"Oh, Maisie," Alice moaned. "It's true!"

"Of course it isn't! Look at this lovely house," Maisie said bravely. "How could it be haunted? It's so beautiful."

But she couldn't help glancing behind her as Annie showed them into the drawing room. The entrance hall was beautiful, but it was full of dark pools of shadow, where the strangest things could be lurking . . .

The delicious lemon cake and the scones that Mrs. James had sent up for tea almost cured Alice of her ghost worries, but not quite. She was still nervous in the big house, and she didn't like walking down the passages without Maisie.

Luckily, the two girls had bedrooms next to each other, with a little door that opened between the two. Maisie was fairly sure that her bedroom was about the size of the whole basement floor of her house at 31 Albion Street. And the huge four-poster bed was bigger than her entire bedroom.

"Good night, Maisie!" Alice called sleepily from the next room. They had decided to keep the little door open so that they could talk to each other, but they were just too tired to chat.

"Good night!" Maisie called back.

Eddie whined and yawned and curled himself into a tiny ball on the old blanket. Annie had found a basket for him in the kitchens, but Maisie was hoping Eddie might decide to sleep on the end of the bed. Her toes were quite chilly.

It was darkest night when Maisie woke
up a few hours later, and at first she
couldn't remember where she was. Even
in the darkness she could tell she wasn't in
her cramped little room at home — the air
smelled different. And there was a strange
noise, not the watchman calling the hours,
or a cab horse trotting home. A wailing
noise . . .

Maisie clutched the blankets around
herself and wriggled up a little, suddenly
remembering that she was in a haunted
house.

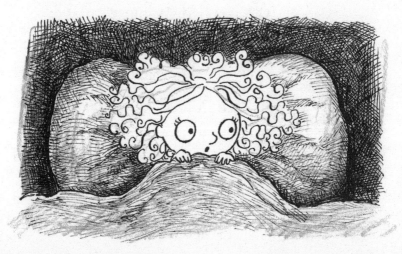

"There's no such thing as ghosts," she
whispered fiercely to herself. Saying it out
loud made her feel more certain somehow.
She reached out for the box of matches,
and her hand shook a little as she lit her
bedroom candle. She held it up, nodding
as she ticked off a list of things that should
be there—Eddie in his basket, the huge
mahogany wardrobe where she'd hung her
few dresses, the darker shape that was the
open doorway to Alice's room.

The wailing noise came again, followed
by a horrified gasp from the room next door.

"Maisie!" Alice sobbed. "A ghost!"

And through the door came a
small white shape, wispy and
thin. A little white ghost cat,
which padded across the
room and disappeared.

Chapter Four

Eddie woke up, snuffling and whining, and
then let out a sharp, surprised bark. He
jumped out of his basket and pattered across
the room to Maisie, with his tail held tightly
against his legs.

Maisie stared at him, her heart thumping.
A ghost cat! She had seen a ghost cat! And
Eddie had seen it too! Then there was a
whispering noise and a little thud, and she

shrank back against the pillows, wondering
what was going to run through her room
next.

A white fluttery shape appeared in the
doorway. Maisie had actually opened her
mouth to scream before she realized it was
only Alice—Alice in her lace-trimmed white
nightgown. Alice, who was even more
scared than she was.

"Did you see it?" she whispered, her teeth chattering.

"Yes. Look, get in with me, you'll freeze." Maisie beckoned her over to the bed and Alice scuttled toward her.

"That was a ghost!"

"Yee-eesss. Maybe." Maisie wasn't quite so sure now. After all, a moment ago, she would have sworn Alice was a ghost too. And who'd ever heard of a phantom cat?

"Maisie, how can you doubt it?" Alice gasped. "The boy was right—and Annie. We both saw it. A real ghost! We must go back to London tomorrow morning. I can't stay here with a ghost!"

Maisie looked at her thoughtfully. "It was only a cat, though. I thought you liked cats."

"Not spectral ones!" Alice shuddered.

"I know it was scary," Maisie murmured,

"but it didn't seem to be a mean ghost . . . If it *was* one, which I still don't believe it was."

"What else could it have been, though?" Alice squeaked indignantly. She sat up and glared at Maisie. "We didn't imagine it!"

"I know . . . and Eddie saw it too." Maisie sighed. "But I don't want to go back to London. Think of all that horrible fog. You won't get better—or not as fast, anyway."

"I think I'd rather be ill than haunted," Alice said, but she sounded uncertain. "Papa was so pleased that he'd found this house for us. He told me before we left that he'd been very worried about me staying in London." She sighed. "You're right, Maisie. We can't go back. Not just because of one little ghost cat, anyway." She gripped Maisie's wrist. "But if a skeleton walks through my bedroom clanking with chains, Maisie

Hitchins, or anything carrying its head under its arm, we're going home that very minute, do you hear? Even if we have to freeze on the station platform all night waiting for a train!"

"Lessons! You can't mean it, Miss Sidebotham!" Alice protested. "I'm ill." She coughed pathetically to prove it, but Maisie had seen the size of the breakfast Alice had eaten, and the governess had too.

"Perhaps not a full morning of lessons then," Miss Sidebotham agreed. "Since you are still recovering. But you can't be allowed to forget all that you've learned, Alice."

"And what's Maisie to do while I'm doing arithmetic and sewing?" Alice asked.

Miss Sidebotham sniffed. "Perhaps she

could help the maids. The house is under-staffed."

Maisie looked down at her plate, embarrassed. It was true that she would usually be doing the sort of things that Annie and Cissie and Lily were doing. She had felt very strange sitting about being waited on. But Miss Sidebotham didn't have to say it in that nasty tone of voice.

"Maisie is a guest! Papa invited her!" Alice snapped indignantly.

Miss Sidebotham gave another of those meaningful sniffs. This one clearly said that Mr. Lacey had been very much misguided.

Maisie twisted her napkin in her fingers and comforted herself that at least she didn't have a name that sounded exactly like Side Bottom. And the bottom to match, even with a corset that was laced so tight, it creaked. The governess was lucky that Alice was far too well behaved to tease her about it. "I can help the maids, Alice," she said quietly. "I could dust our rooms, at least."

"Good." Miss Sidebotham nodded triumphantly. Then she patted the frills at the front of her dress and frowned. "My spectacles! Now, where on earth are they? Have either of you girls seen them?"

Alice shook her head and looked gloomily into what was left of her porridge.

Maisie looked at the governess thoughtfully. Miss Sidebotham usually wore her little pince-nez spectacles on a fussy gold chain, so that they hung around her neck when they weren't perched on the end of her nose.

"I haven't seen them, Miss Sidebotham," she said, shaking her head. "Not since yesterday, I'm sure."

"I must have left them in my room. Alice, I have left your books on the table in the lilac parlor, where we shall have our lessons. Go and cast an eye over your Latin vocabulary while I find my spectacles."

Maisie was in the hallway with Eddie, admiring the chandelier and thinking about going down to the kitchens to ask for a duster and some furniture polish, when Miss Sidebotham came hurrying down the marble staircase.

"Maisie! When did you say you saw my spectacles?" she snapped.

"You were wearing them when we had dinner, miss," Maisie told her. "You couldn't find them upstairs?"

"No! Someone has taken them! That gold chain was a present from one of my previous employers, and it is most valuable. I *know* I left the spectacles in the china tray on the dressing table in my room. Someone must have stolen them!" Miss Sidebotham was scarlet with rage and practically shouting.

Alice popped her head out of the lilac parlor. Maisie wondered if the maids could hear from down in the kitchens.

"It must have been that insolent girl who

answered the door to us yesterday. She lit the fire in my bedroom this morning, and she woke me, quite deliberately, clattering the fire irons about."

"If she was going to steal your gold chain, miss, she wouldn't want to wake you," Maisie pointed out. "She'd want you to stay asleep in case you saw her take the chain."

"Don't be so impertinent!" Miss Sidebotham snapped. "Of course it was her. Unless *you* took them *yourself,* which wouldn't surprise me in the least."

Maisie gaped at her, shocked. She had never been accused of stealing before, and she didn't know what to say.

"Maisie isn't a thief!" Alice cried, running out into the hallway. "She's a detective!"

"Nonsense." Miss Sidebotham looked

crosser than ever, and when Annie came into the hallway from the kitchens, the governess glared at her.

"Is anything wrong, miss?" Annie asked. "We heard a . . . a disturbance."

"Did you indeed?" Miss Sidebotham sniffed again. "Yes, there most certainly is something wrong. My spectacles—and the gold chain attached to them—have disappeared."

"Oh dear, miss." Annie said. "Could they have fallen off your dressing table?"

"So you knew that's where I had put them?" Miss Sidebotham snapped.

"Well, yes, miss. I saw them when I came in to light your bedroom fire this morning. The dressing table's by the window, you see. If you remember, you asked me last night to open the window for you in the morning. Quite determined about it, you were."

"Fresh air is most important," Miss Sidebotham said, nodding.

"That's as may be, miss, but that window stuck something dreadful. Not been opened in years, I'd say. So I was rattling away at it, right next to the dressing table. Of course I saw your spectacles."

"Hmmm." Miss Sidebotham still sounded suspicious, and Annie frowned back at her.

"Why, miss? You're not suggesting I took them, are you?"

The governess folded her arms and looked down her nose at Annie—which was quite difficult, as she was considerably shorter than the maid. "You are the only person who has been in my room."

"Well!" Annie folded her arms too, and glared so furiously that Miss Sidebotham stepped back, nearly falling over Eddie. "I never heard the like. Calling me a thief! I'm not staying here to be treated like this." She started to undo the ties at the back of her apron, as if she intended to throw it on the floor and march out of the house there and then.

"Please don't go, Annie." Alice hurried forward. "Miss Sidebotham, I'm sure we'll find your spectacles. It must be a mistake. They must have fallen down the back of the dressing table or something." She ushered her governess over to one of the little chairs, murmuring, "Don't worry." Then she came over to Maisie and Annie and added in a whisper, "I don't suppose Eddie . . . ?"

Maisie looked down at the little dog, who stared back at her with one paw held up and his ears quivering, as though Miss Sidebotham had dealt him a blow. She shook her head. "He hasn't been in her room, I'm sure of it. I bet she's lost them herself."

Annie pulled a handkerchief out of the pocket of her apron and dabbed at her eyes, although Maisie couldn't see if she was actually crying. "Such a shock . . . To be called a thief like that. I'm not sure I can stay here to be insulted . . ."

Maisie patted her arm comfortingly. "It's just a misunderstanding, Annie, that's all." She glanced at Alice. If Miss Sidebotham upset Annie again, she was clearly going to flounce off and leave, which would make it even more difficult for the other maids

to look after this huge house. Maisie didn't
mind helping out, but the whole point of her
being here was to keep Alice company. She
could do dusting at home.

"I hope so," Annie said tearfully. "It's
bad enough as it is, with all these strange
goings-on."

"What strange goings-on?" Alice asked in
a horrified voice.

"That's what I was coming to tell you,
miss. Cissie and Lily say there's a dreadful
smell coming from the library. They went to
take off the dust sheets and air it out, seeing
as your governess said that you'd want to
use it."

"Do we?" Alice asked, looking at Miss
Sidebotham in surprise.

"For your lessons, Alice! It will be most
useful," the governess said. "It can't be that

hard to take off the covers and light a fire! I am going upstairs to keep looking for my spectacles." She swept away crossly and Maisie sighed, exchanging an understanding look with Annie.

"It isn't just the smell, miss . . ." Annie said in a doom-laden voice. "Noxious vapors, they say there was. Like a green fog. And then a terrible screeching noise, echoing about the room. The two of them came running back down to the kitchens shrieking as though they were being murdered." She looked around at them smugly, enjoying having an audience. "And they say they won't go back in there even for double wages," she added in triumph.

"Where is the library?" Maisie asked. She still wasn't sure where half the rooms were.

"Over on that side of the hall, miss.

Down the passage," Annie explained. "There's a couple of small parlors and the billiards room down there too. It's all been shut up, though."

"Let's go and see," Maisie said, picking up Eddie for moral support and marching off down the passage with Alice and Annie following after her.

"Do we have to?" Alice whispered as they padded along—the corridor was quite dark, as all the windows had shutters over them, and portraits loomed out of the shadows in a most nerve-racking way.

"It's probably just a dead mouse," Maisie pointed out. "We had one once, behind a wardrobe in Madame Lorimer's rooms—it stunk the place out."

"That wouldn't explain the noxious vapors, though." Annie shook her head.

"Rising out of the floorboards, Cissie said they were."

Alice gasped, but Maisie gave Annie a doubtful look. "Are you sure?"

"Well, I didn't see them myself, of course," Annie admitted. "But there was the screeching as well, don't forget. There's something unearthly in that room, miss. Or under it . . ."

"What's that supposed to mean?" Maisie demanded as they reached the library door. A pile of cleaning things lay abandoned just outside, where the maids had left them as they'd run away, and even though Maisie was trying hard not to believe in ghosts, the gaping doorway made her shudder.

"This house is haunted, miss, I'm certain of it," Annie said as they peered cautiously around the door. The library looked

perfectly normal now—only as spooky
as any dimly lit room with the furniture
covered in dust sheets. "There, can't you
smell it?"

Maisie and Alice sniffed, and Alice started to cough horribly. "Oh, that's disgusting. Maisie, that can't just be a dead mouse."

"A rat maybe . . ." Maisie muttered. It really was a dreadful smell—so bad, it felt like she could see it seeping out of the floor and taste it coating the back of her throat.

"It's the dead, miss . . ." Annie moaned dramatically. "Rising up out of their graves!"

Chapter Five

Maisie and Alice had decided most
definitively that they did not need to use the
library.

"Imagine sitting in there!" Alice
whispered to Maisie as they helped Annie
carry the dusters and sweeping brush back
along the passage and down to the kitchens.
"You'd always be wondering what it was
creeping up behind your chair and putting

its cold fingers on your neck . . ."

"Oh, don't, miss!" Annie moaned. "This house is built on a graveyard — everyone says so . . ."

Maisie sighed. Annie was a born gossip, she thought. And she was doing a very good job of frightening Alice to death.

"I still think it was a dead rat," she said firmly.

"Maybe it's a ghost rat now, like the ghost cat we saw!" Alice said suddenly, dropping the dustpan so it clattered down the kitchen stairs, and staring at Maisie in horror.

"You actually saw a ghost, miss?" Annie gasped and the two other maids came out of the kitchen, looking terrified.

"She saw it?"

"Ooohhh, I can't stay here! Not with all those dreadful shrieking noises . . ." The youngest of the maids was in tears, and she was actually shaking. "They made my skin creep, miss, and now you've seen a real ghost! I can't stay here, I just can't."

The cook, a tiny lady in a print dress and an apron all covered in flour, came hurrying out after them. "What? You've seen it?"

"It was just a little white cat—" Maisie started to say, but no one was listening to her. Mrs. James was having the vapors and being held up by Annie and one of the other maids. The youngest maid, Lily, was kneeling on the floor and calling on the soul of her dead grandmother to save her from this evil house.

Even Alice looked slightly surprised by the scene she'd set off. "Please don't cry," she murmured to Mrs. James, but it was no good.

"I can't stay here to be murdered in my bed by ghosts!" the cook gasped. "No one said anything about hauntings when I took the job! I'm leaving—now!"

"And me!" both Lily and Cissie chimed in and Annie nodded grimly, "Me too."

"But you can't!" Maisie gasped. "You've had wages in advance. And you have to give notice, surely, so we can find someone else?"

"You won't. No one's going to want to work here," Annie pointed out. "Not when we tell them what it's like. And ghosts weren't mentioned when we were engaged, like Mrs. James said. False pretenses, that is. I'm going to pack." And she marched away up the stairs, with the others following after her.

"This is ridiculous . . ." Maisie muttered. "I don't believe this house is haunted at all. The boy at the station said the last people asked the vicar about a plague pit and he told them it was nonsense."

"But the cat . . ." Alice reminded her. "I suppose the smell could just be a dead rat. But we both saw the cat and so did Eddie. Perhaps we should write to Papa and ask him to fetch us home?"

"Well, we haven't come across a skeleton yet," Maisie reminded her.

"I suppose so . . ." Alice agreed reluctantly. "But what are we going to do without any servants?"

Maisie thought. "Have you ever done any cooking?"

Alice shook her head. "No. Well, only gingerbread elephants. I'm allowed to sit on the edge of the kitchen table and watch our cook." She giggled. "She lets me hide from Miss Sidebotham sometimes."

"We might need a bit more than gingerbread . . ." Maisie said. "I wonder where Miss Sidebotham is. I'd have thought she'd have come searching for you by now. Maybe she's still hunting for her spectacles."

Maisie tiptoed into the kitchen and peered at the pans bubbling on the stove. "Well, it looks like we'll get our lunch, at least," she said. "I know how to use a stove like this, I think. It isn't all that different from the one my gran has. Just bigger." She wandered around the kitchen, looking at the boards full of chopped vegetables and the mound of washing-up piled in the scullery next door. "I suppose at least there's only the three of us now," she said thoughtfully. "Mrs. James was having to cook for seven. And all the food must be delivered from the shops in the village. I should think there's enough in here for the rest of the week," she added, peeping into the huge stone-floored larder. "Look at all that cheese! And there's a side of bacon, eggs, everything!"

"Maisie, do you actually think we can cook for ourselves?" Alice asked doubtfully.

"I can't make calves'-foot jelly . . ." Maisie told her apologetically.

Alice smiled. "Thank goodness."

"It won't be the sort of thing Mrs. Daley serves you at home, or like that delicious dinner Mrs. James sent upstairs yesterday. No French cuisine, no Sweetbreads à la Maître d'Hôtel."

Alice shuddered. "I don't mind. Sweetbreads aren't what they sound like at all. Can we do this washing-up? It looks quite fun."

Maisie looked at the pile and sighed. "I think I'd better wash. Miss Sidebotham would have forty fits if you reddened your hands. There's some boiling water in the copper—it's still steaming hot. You can dry. I saw aprons somewhere. Oh, here look." She pulled two out of a drawer in the dresser and they put them on. Alice was giggling as though it was an adventure and Maisie couldn't help laughing too. It was

hard to imagine someone who had never
washed up in her life. She watched Alice
anxiously as she handed her the pretty china
teacups, but Alice was actually far more
careful than she was.

"My gran would say you're a good worker," she told Alice approvingly, and her friend went pink with pleasure.

"Do you think Miss Sidebotham will be cross?" Alice asked as she dried another plate.

Maisie shrugged. "She doesn't have much choice, does she? Not if she wants to eat. But once she knows the servants have gone, I should think she'll write to your father. Or maybe even telegraph him. And I doubt if she'll be much use in the kitchen."

Alice sighed. "I suppose so."

"Girls! Girls! Alice, where are you?" A thin, frightened voice echoed down from the main part of the house — it was Miss Sidebotham. Maisie and Alice exchanged looks and hurried through the servants' quarters, pulling off the aprons as they went.

"What is it?" Alice asked anxiously, after they found Miss Sidebotham tottering down the last steps of the marble staircase. She was horribly pale and had her handkerchief pressed against her lips as though she felt sick. "You still can't find your spectacles?"

"Spectacles . . ." the governess whimpered. "I have just seen a specter!" And she fainted to the floor.

Miss Sidebotham was laid out on the drawing room sofa with her handkerchief, smelling salts, and a little brass bell she had found on the mantelpiece. She kept ringing it to call Alice and Maisie to bring her cups of tea and anchovy paste sandwiches, both of which, luckily, were quite easy to make.

It was a phantom cat that she had seen, she had explained, when she was well enough to talk. Apparently it had flitted down the upstairs corridor, outside her room, and frightened her into a fit. When the girls told her that the servants had walked out, she went into what she called a nervous collapse.

"I thought ghosts only came out at night," Maisie said to Alice as she cut bread for sandwiches and fed the trimmed crusts to Eddie. Miss Sidebotham liked them crustless—she was very particular about her sandwiches, they'd found.

"I hadn't thought of that," Alice said, frowning as she stirred the tea in the pot. "Perhaps the cat is ever such a powerful ghost . . . Oh drat! That's Miss Sidebotham's bell again!"

"Well, she'll just have to wait! Honestly, she's your governess and she's got you running around after her like a slave. You're supposed to be resting."

Alice nodded. "I know. But I do feel so much better already, away from that dreadful fog. And this is fun."

The bell jangled again and Alice and Maisie carried the tea and sandwiches up to the drawing room.

"Oh! There you are at last! I feel quite

dreadfully faint again. It's too cold in here. You must light the fire," Miss Sidebotham commanded in a feeble voice.

Maisie shook her head disgustedly, noticing that she was quite well enough to wolf down the sandwiches. "We aren't doing any more tea after this," she said sternly. "I'll light the fire, but then we have to finish getting the lunch. You'll have to put more coal on yourself." She went over to the fireplace, ignoring Miss Sidebotham's shocked mutterings about her manners, and knelt down to light the fire. The maids

had left it laid with kindling—she only needed to set a match to it and add a little coal.

"There," she said, standing up, and then she coughed a little.

"Oh! It's smoking terribly. You can't have lit it properly, you silly girl!" snapped Miss Sidebotham.

Maisie felt like telling her to do it herself, but the fire *was* smoking, which was odd, as she was very used to lighting fires at home. The sweetish blue-gray smoke wafted out of the fireplace, swirling around the room and setting them all coughing. Maisie had a go at it with the poker, but it only seemed to make it worse. "Open a window," she called to Alice, but Alice was standing transfixed in the middle of the room.

"Maisie, look!" she whispered in horror. Maisie turned round from the fireplace to see the ghost cat trotting towards her, its green eyes shining through the veils of smoke.

Eddie growled and the fur rose up on the back of his neck. He stepped toward the ghost, but it ignored him, turning away from the fire and walking towards the corner of the room. Its glimmering white tail wafted from side to side and it brushed across Maisie's hand as it padded past. Then it went on through the wisps of smoke and disappeared. Maisie shivered in horror.

"It's a sign!" wailed Miss Sidebotham. "We're not long for this world. We're all cursed!"

"Oh, Maisie, it touched you," Alice whispered, her blue eyes round and frightened.

"I know . . ." Maisie said, staring down at her hand.

"Did it hurt you?" Alice gasped, hurrying

over to look. "Has it burned you, or something awful like that?"

"No." Maisie shook her head. Now she thought about it, it hadn't hurt her at all. And it hadn't been hot, or icy, or even damp. It had felt just like any other cat—soft and warm and furry. Maisie had a feeling it wasn't a ghost at all!

Chapter Six

"It's just a cat!" Maisie told Alice again. "It seemed quite friendly to me. It's probably lived here for ages."

"Yes, hundreds of years!" Alice said, nodding her head stubbornly. "No one mentioned a cat when we arrived. If there was a cat in the house, wouldn't someone have had to feed it? It would come into the kitchens to be fed. When we said that we'd seen a white cat it wouldn't have frightened away Annie and the others, would it? They'd have told us not to be silly and that it was only the kitchen cat!"

"I suppose so," Maisie murmured. They were walking around the gardens, exercising Eddie, while Miss Sidebotham had a rest on the sofa. Maisie thought she was probably sleeping off lunch. Mrs. James had prepared plenty, and somehow the encounter with the not-a-ghost-cat had left everyone feeling very hungry. "Actually, I bet it smelled Miss Sidebotham's sandwiches!" she said suddenly. "Cats love fish, don't they? I should think anchovy paste sandwiches would be a real treat. Perhaps it just lives on mice. It looked ever so thin, poor thing."

"Well, who ever heard of a fat ghost?" Alice said, throwing a stick for Eddie, so he

raced off across the grass, barking excitedly.
He wasn't used to such nice places to play
in. Playing with him had reddened Alice's
cheeks too, and brightened her eyes. She
looked worlds better. And not as worried
about the phantom cat, either, now that
Maisie had touched it and lived to tell the
tale.

"I suppose it could be a friendly ghost," Alice said thoughtfully. "It hasn't done anything awful . . ."

"Actually, it's done you a favor," Maisie pointed out. "Miss Sidebotham's far too upset about being haunted to think about lessons now."

Alice laughed. "You're right, I hadn't thought of that. It's fun staying here and looking after ourselves, Maisie. If she writes a letter to Papa, I think we should—er—lose it . . ."

"Alice Honoria Lacey!" Maisie said, grinning. "Miss Sidebotham's right. I *am* a bad influence on you."

"Maisie, have you seen my silver bracelet?" Alice asked worriedly, coming into Maisie's room as they were getting ready for bed that night.

"What, the pretty one you always wear, with the little sparkly flowers?" Maisie asked.

"Yes, I can't find it—I took it off because I thought it would get in the way with the cooking and the washing up. I'm sure I put it on the kitchen windowsill, but I just went back downstairs to fetch it and it's gone."

Maisie shook her head. "No, I haven't seen it anywhere. You're really sure you left it there?"

"Definitely." Alice looked at Maisie, frowning anxiously. "Do you think it's another ghost? Miss Sidebotham would say it was one of the servants, but it can't have been. I definitely had it on until lunchtime, and they'd all left by then."

Maisie snorted. "Or she'd say it was me."

"Yes, but I know it wasn't you." Alice nibbled one of her nails. "So it must have been a ghost . . ."

"Why would a ghost want your bracelet?" Maisie asked, but even she felt a little worried. Miss Sidebotham's spectacles still hadn't turned up, and now the bracelet had disappeared as well. There was definitely something odd going on. "I don't think ghosts steal things," she said, trying to sound as though she believed it.

"But there's no one else here!" Alice glanced nervously from side to side, as though she expected ghosts to come creeping out from behind the curtains. "I'm not sure I can stay here after all, Maisie . . . It must be another ghost. Who knows how many of them there are?"

Maisie sighed. "Well, Miss Sidebotham

said she was going to write to your father. She told me I have to take the letter into the village tomorrow to post it."

Alice sighed. "I just don't know what to do—I do like it here, but I keep thinking something awful's going to happen . . ."

The next morning, Maisie hurried down the driveway with Miss Sidebotham's letter in her hand and Eddie trotting beside her. She and Alice had talked it over and decided that they ought to post the letter. Neither the bracelet nor the spectacles had turned up, and the dreadful smell from the library side of the house seemed to be getting stronger.

Miss Sidebotham's letter told Mr. Lacey that the house was mostly definitely haunted and probably built on the site of some dreadful battle. She added that she could not be held responsible for the girls' safety.

"As if that little cat had actually done anything to us," Maisie told Eddie with a sigh. "Goodness, it's cold." There was a biting wind, swooshing through the tall trees that lined the drive. "Those nests don't look very safe," Maisie murmured, glancing up at the loose bundles of sticks up above her head. "Oh, a magpie. *One for sorrow* . . . We don't need any more bad luck, thank you." More of the black and white birds swooped down to land in the trees, chattering and squawking, and Maisie sighed happily. It was only a silly rhyme, of course, but still . . . "There's lots of them, that's all right. *Seven for a secret, never to be told* . . . I wonder what it is."

She hurried on down the drive and turned onto the road that ran through the village. Only a few minutes later, she could see the church spire up above her, and she came to the main village street.

Maisie looked around, wondering where the post box would be. She was just deciding that she would have to ask someone—there was a cluster of people standing outside the greengrocer's shop—when one of the women walked over to her.

"Good morning, miss."

"Oh! Hello, Annie. I didn't recognize you for a minute." The maid looked very different in her neat dark coat and hat instead of her uniform.

"How are you, miss? Have you and Miss Alice seen any more ghosts?"

Maisie looked at her carefully, trying to work out if she was serious or not. Her voice sounded as though she was really most anxious to know, but there was a hint of a smirk at the corner of her mouth.

"No . . . Well, we did see the ghost cat again. And the smell is getting worse . . ." she admitted. She didn't feel like mentioning the bracelet. Annie had been so cross with Miss Sidebotham about her spectacles and Maisie didn't want to offend her.

"Oh dear . . ." Annie was definitely trying not to smile, Maisie was sure of it. She thought it was funny! "I do hope that

Miss Sidebotham isn't too upset about it all," Annie cooed sweetly.

"Could you tell me where to find the post box, please?" Maisie asked, trying not to sound too cross.

"Just over there, miss," Annie said pointing. "Important letter home, is it?" She peered at the address on the letter in Maisie's hand. "To Miss Alice's father?"

"Yes." Maisie scowled. "Miss Sidebotham has written to tell him about the strange goings-on in the house."

"Oh, is that so?" Annie was smiling widely, and Maisie stalked away to the post box without saying goodbye. She was sure now that Annie hadn't believed in the ghost at all. She had probably been angry that Miss Sidebotham had accused her of stealing and then had convinced everyone the ghost story was true, just to pay the governess back!

Maisie marched back to Wisteria Lodge with a determined look on her face. She was certain now that the ghosts were just a bunch of silly stories. And she was going to prove it.

Unfortunately, she had absolutely no idea how . . .

"How dare she?" Alice squeaked, after Maisie told her about the meeting with Annie. She banged her hands crossly into the bread dough she was kneading. "Oh, Maisie, you shouldn't have posted that letter! Now Papa will make us come home, for no reason at all."

"I know," Maisie agreed. "I almost didn't post it, but then I thought about the smell. I can't think what's causing it, but I bet it isn't good for you. And there are those shrieking noises—when I woke up this morning, I'd been dreaming that there was a ghost screaming in my ear. I jumped out of bed and then I saw that Eddie was awake too, whining, and the fur on the back of his neck was sticking up. I think there really *was* a strange noise, even if it wasn't a ghost. I heard it while I was asleep and it went into my dream. So I want to find out what it is.

Besides, if we solve the mystery, we can write again and tell your father we can stay, can't we?"

"You should have woken me up and told me!" Alice said. "I'm always moaning to you about things. Urrgh. This means we have to go back to the library," she added, shuddering. "Even though I'm almost sure the ghosts were all made up, I still don't want to. It's so spooky in there."

"You don't have to come—" Maisie started to say, but Alice glared at her.

"Of course I'm coming with you! Eddie and I are your faithful assistants." She pulled off her apron and looked rather doubtfully at the bread dough. "Do you think that looks right? It's ever such an odd grayish color."

Maisie thought it looked dreadful, but she decided not to say so. "I'm sure it always looks like that before it's baked."

"Maybe . . . Come on then!" Alice started to walk bravely out of the kitchen, but she turned back before she reached the door to grab Maisie's hand.

The smell got worse and worse as they started down the passage from the entrance hall to the library. It was almost choking and the darkness of the passage made it seem even harder to breathe. They had brought a candle with them from the kitchen, but it didn't burn very brightly.

"It's dreadful!" Maisie coughed, pulling out her handkerchief and pressing it to her nose as they reached the open library door.

"Are there any green mists rising out of the floor?" Alice asked as they peered into the dim room.

"Not that I can see . . ." Maisie told her.
"Oh, Eddie, come back!"

The little dog had pricked up his ears and
then dashed into the room, barking loudly.

"It's the phantom cat!" Alice clutched
Maisie's arm. "Look, there it is, walking along
the back of the sofa! Eddie, don't chase it, it
might do something awful to you!"

"Eddie!" Maisie yelled, but he was far too excited to listen. He never did listen when he was chasing cats, she remembered, thinking of that time on the way to Alice's house a few days before.

The ghost cat saw Eddie hurtling toward it. It took a flying leap off the sofa and disappeared behind one of the huge

bookcases that stuck out into the room. Eddie went after it.

Maisie forgot the awfulness of the smell and ran after them. *That* was no ghost! Surely a ghost cat wouldn't need to run away? If Eddie tried to catch a ghost cat, he'd just run straight through it, wouldn't he? And a ghost cat wouldn't smell like a proper cat either, so Eddie probably wouldn't want to chase it anyway.

I should have thought of that before, Maisie told herself crossly. *He's behaving just like he did with that cat in the street.* It was a real cat, this proved it for sure.

She hurried around the bookcase, expecting to find Eddie and the cat hissing and scratching at each other, or maybe the cat halfway up the long velvet curtains that were draped behind the bookcase. Then she stopped in surprise and Alice caught up with her. Eddie and the cat had completely disappeared.

"Where is he?" Alice asked, and then she gave a horrified gasp. "Oh, Maisie, that ghost cat's eaten Eddie!"

"It can't have done," Maisie murmured, running her fingers along the bookcase and frowning. "Eddie didn't think that cat was a ghost and neither do I. They've just gone — somewhere."

There was a scuttling, scratching noise from behind the bookshelf, and both girls took a step back, clutching each other's hands. A black nose appeared around the edge of the bookcase, and Alice took in a panicked breath. Then Eddie came out into the library, looking grumpy.

"Eddie!" Both girls rushed to hug him, but even that didn't seem to cheer him up. His ears had gone back to being flat and floppy again, and his eyes were gloomy. "Did that cat get away, Eddie?" Maisie said, patting him. "You shouldn't chase them anyway. But where did you go?" She stood up and went to look around the edge of the bookcase, pushing the curtain out of the way.

A narrow, dark gap opened out behind the bookcase—just big enough for a slim person to slip through.

"Alice! Look! A secret passage!" Maisie poked her head in, holding up the candle so she could look around. "It must lead to the floor above—there's a little staircase. So this is how that white cat kept appearing and disappearing all over the place! There must be passages like this all over the house!"

Alice shuddered. "Ooohh. I don't like the sound of that—people could creep up on us all the time."

"I suppose so," Maisie agreed. "But it's very clever. I'm going to see where it goes."

Alice gulped, but she and Eddie followed Maisie into the black gap and up the winding wooden stairs.

Chapter Seven

The stairway grew lighter as they went
farther up, and the awful smell cleared away
too. "We must be getting up toward the
first floor," Maisie whispered back to Alice.
"There aren't any shutters over the windows
up here, so that's why it's lighter. I wonder
where the passage comes out?"

"I hope it's soon," Alice whispered.
"There are spider webs everywhere. I keep

thinking I can feel little legs in my hair."

Maisie stopped suddenly as she reached
a flat wooden panel with only a narrow strip
of light down the side—just wide enough
for a very thin cat to push its way through.

Eddie sniffed at it excitedly, and as Maisie
held the candle closer, she could see white
hairs caught on the side of the panel. She
hooked her fingers around it and pushed.
The wooden panel creaked and stuck,
then slid farther across, leaving a narrow
doorway.

"Look, it's my bedroom!" Maisie gasped
as she pushed the panel aside. "We've come
out just behind that massive wardrobe!"

They stepped out into the room and
Maisie looked back at the door, trying to
work out how she'd missed a secret doorway
in her own bedroom. She blew out the

candle and set it down by her bed, then went to investigate.

"Oh! You can't see the opening unless the door's pulled across all the way," she said, pulling at the sliding panel. "When it was only open enough for the cat to get through, the open part was still behind the wardrobe."

"And the cat could squeeze out under the bottom of the wardrobe, I suppose," Alice agreed. "Oh, look, it's still here!"

The white cat was in the doorway between Maisie's room and Alice's, looking back at them curiously. But as soon as it spotted Eddie again, it darted away.

"Let's follow it!" Maisie said, dashing across the room with Eddie. "I want to see if there are any more secret passages. I bet that cat knows them all!"

The cat whisked around the door and

into the passage that led one way to the
stairs and the other way to the warren of
empty bedrooms that the girls hadn't had
time to explore properly. The white cat
flitted through a half-open door, and Eddie
and Maisie and Alice piled after it.

The room had pretty pale pink wallpaper,
printed with little flowers. The curtains
tied back on the four-poster bed were pink
to match. It reminded Maisie of Alice's
bedroom back in London.

Eddie raced across the dusty wooden floor after the cat, but for the first time it stood its ground instead of running away from him. It stopped in front of the big wooden wardrobe that stood in the corner of the room, arched its back, and hissed.

Maisie and Alice stopped in surprise. Even Eddie skidded to a halt and stared at it. In his experience, cats ran—they didn't fight back.

The cat's whiskers were bristling and its green eyes were slitted and furious.

Eddie glanced uncertainly at Maisie, then took a step toward the wardrobe.

The cat shot out a paw and raked its claws across Eddie's nose.

He whimpered and scuttled back to Maisie, with three red, oozing lines across his nose. The cat jumped through the half-open door of the wardrobe.

"Maybe there's another secret passage in there," Maisie said doubtfully. She couldn't work out why the cat had suddenly been so angry. It hadn't tried to attack Eddie until they came into this particular room.

"No, listen . . ." Alice edged toward the wardrobe, her eyes shining with excitement. "Can't you hear?"

Maisie followed her, with Eddie squashed worriedly up against her boots. "What is it? I can hear something squeaking, I think . . . Oh, has it caught a mouse?"

"No, silly!" Alice peeped inside. "Kittens!" She crouched down. "Oh, aren't they beautiful . . . Aren't you a clever cat!"

"They're not ghost kittens, then?" Maisie asked her, grinning, but Alice wasn't listening. She was too busy whispering endearments to the two kittens and their mother. The white cat looked at Alice suspiciously over her babies, but she seemed to understand that this girl didn't mean them any harm.

Eddie whined crossly. He didn't see why all this attention was being paid to the white cat, when it had meanly scratched him. Maisie picked him up and rubbed his ears comfortingly. "I know, it isn't fair, is it? But she must have thought you were going to hurt her kittens." She carried Eddie over to an armchair by the window and curled up on top of the dust cover to cuddle him.

"We've solved our ghost mystery, Eddie," she murmured. "Some of it, anyway. A white cat hiding up here doesn't explain the graveyard smell. Or the shrieking noises Cissie and Lily said they heard in the library. I don't think they were lying, like Annie was. They really did look scared. And I'm sure I did hear something this morning. It was all mixed up in my dream, though. This is such a strange house. I just don't know what's real . . ."

Maisie gazed out of the window, trying
to think what the explanation could be. She
refused to believe in ghosts and graveyards,
but the smell was definitely getting worse.
She could even get a little hint of it all the
way up here. Maybe she should open the
window and let some fresh air in?

Maisie knelt up on the armchair and
pulled at the window catch. It was very stiff
and the window seemed to be stuck. She
tried giving it a shove and
then noticed that there was
a wodge of folded
paper stuck into the
side of the frame,
holding it shut. It
must have been
rattling. Maisie

yanked the paper out and the window
opened jerkily. She sat down again, cuddling
Eddie for warmth—the fresh air was nice,
but the room was chilly. She'd have to
shut the window when they went back
downstairs, or the kittens would freeze.

Alice was still sitting in front of the
wardrobe, telling the white cat how clever
she was and how beautiful her kittens were.

"Maisie, is there any fish in the larder?"
she asked hopefully, looking around. "This
poor cat is so thin and her kittens are getting
quite big. She needs feeding up and they
must need proper food too, I think."

"Miss Sidebotham's eaten all the anchovy
paste. But I think there were some kippers,"
Maisie said. "Do cats like kippers?"

"Oh, I'm sure they do!"

Maisie sighed. She hated kippers—but

129

perhaps the kipper whiff would hide the awful smell from the library. "I'll go and cook them, then, shall I?"

Alice beamed at her. "Would you really? Thank you, Maisie!"

Maisie wandered back down the stairs to the kitchen. She shushed Eddie and crept carefully past the drawing room door so as not to be ambushed by Miss Sidebotham and ordered to make more sandwiches. It would be tricky anyway, as she wasn't at all convinced by Alice's bread making.

Maisie got the kippers out of the larder—nasty, leathery, bony things, they were. The cat was welcome to them. She went to look at the stove—Alice had let it die down a bit, not being used to having to look after a fire. Maisie added some more coal and looked at it hopefully. She needed it to burn up, to get hot enough to boil the water for jugging the kippers. If only they had some newspaper, she could put it over the front of the grate to get the fire to draw up. Maisie looked around the kitchen, but she couldn't see any—and then she remembered the wodge of paper from the window. She pulled it out of her pocket and started to unfold it, then sighed. It wasn't newspaper—it was an old letter, and the sheets of paper were far too small to lay over the bars of the grate. Maisie was just about to throw the paper on the fire when a few words caught her eye.

DREADFUL SMELL, REALLY QUITE CHOKING

Maisie wasn't sure if it was right to read other people's letters, but she was a detective, after all. She wasn't just being nosy. She opened the letter properly and frowned at the spiky writing. It made her think that the person who wrote the letter had been cross, stabbing the pen at the paper and leaving blots here and there.

> WE HAVE BEEN LET THIS HOUSE UNDER FALSE PRETENSES AND I WISH TO COMPLAIN MOST STRONGLY. CLEARLY THERE IS SOMETHING WRONG WITH THE DRAINS AND THE CESSPIT IS BLOCKED. I ONLY HOPE THAT WE SHALL NOT ALL SUCCUMB TO SOME INFECTIOUS DISEASE. WISTERIA LODGE SHOULD NEVER HAVE BEEN LET IN THIS STATE. IT IS A MOST DREADFUL SMELL, REALLY QUITE CHOKING. WE SHALL BE LEAVING TODAY AND I REQUIRE THE RETURN OF OUR RENT, AT ONCE.

The drains! Of course! Maisie nodded to herself. This must have been a letter to the house agent, from one of the last people to rent the house. Perhaps the letter writer had made a neater copy afterward. This one was very hard to read, with lots of angry cross-outs and blots all over it.

How could they have been so stupid? It was all that boy's fault, filling their heads with ghosts before they even got to the house. They had never thought of the simple explanation for the terrible smell, or the phantom cat.

Maisie folded her arms, frowning. That only left the shrieking noises and the strange disappearance of Alice's bracelet and Miss Sidebotham's spectacles. It was time to solve the last part of the mystery.

Chapter Eight

"Maisie! Maisie!"

"Sorry I took so long!" Maisie hurried up the rest of the stairs to Alice. "I've brought some kipper, but the cat's going to have to eat round the bones. I'm dreadful at getting them out. Oh, whatever's the matter?" Maisie stopped as she saw her friend shaking on the landing.

"Maisie, didn't you hear it?"

"No." Maisie stared at her. "No, I didn't hear a thing. What was it?"

"Screams! The most awful screams! Like you heard this morning, Maisie. They were like a soul in torment! Maybe Annie was right about the graveyard, after all."

"She wasn't," Maisie said firmly. "I've just found a letter complaining about the state of the drains. That's all the smell is. Drains. Or lack of them, I suppose. There must be an explanation for the noises, too."

"Oh . . . do you think so?" Alice asked. Maisie wondered if she had been enjoying being scared, just a little. She sounded a bit disappointed that Maisie was so matter-of-fact.

"Yes. Where did they come from? Oh, here, you'd better give this to the cat. Eddie's desperate for it." She handed a rather pretty

china plate full of kipper to Alice. Eddie's
tail drooped sadly.

"Oh, she'll be so pleased!" Alice glanced
up. "Must we really go and look for whatever
made that noise? I think it was in the attics.
It definitely came from above me."

"The attic stairs are along here, I think,"
Maisie said. "Past the cat's room. You give
her the fish, then we'll go and look upstairs."

Alice gulped and darted off to put the plate down in front of the wardrobe. Maisie held on to Eddie, who whined pitifully, as though no one had ever given him so much as a whitebait.

"Shhh," Maisie told him. "I'll give you something much, much nicer when we've found out what's making those noises. You did help us solve our ghost mystery, after all."

Alice tiptoed reluctantly back into the passage, and when Maisie opened the door up to the servants' rooms and the attic stairs, she shuddered. "I suppose we must . . ." she whispered as she followed Maisie.

The attic floor was enormous, much larger than the attics back at Maisie's house in London. They were full of broken furniture, dusty old paintings, and trunks packed with old clothes. Maisie would have

liked to explore properly, and Alice cried out
with delight at a box full of old hats, trailing
faded feathers and wisps of net.

"We can look later," Maisie said firmly.
"We have to find where the noise came
from first. Maybe it was just a creaking door,
blowing in the wind?"

"It was not a door, Maisie," Alice said
firmly. "You wouldn't say that if you'd heard

it. And why would the doors creak anyway? The windows up here aren't open."

"Hmm. I suppose not . . . It *is* chilly, though." Maisie shivered. "Maybe the draft comes down the chimney."

Just then, the most unearthly shrieking noise echoed around the room, a shrill wail that stopped Maisie's breath and made her and Alice clutch at each other in panic.

"Let's go! Let's go!" Alice whimpered, and even Eddie cowered against the two girls as though he thought something awful was coming after them all.

"Wait!" Maisie gasped. "I don't believe in ghosts! I don't!" she muttered to herself—though it was very hard to be sure, with the echoes of that dreadful shriek still in her ears. "There's been an explanation for the other things," she whispered shakily. "There must be an explanation for this, too." She took a step toward the fireplace. "Do you think it came from over there?"

"Maybe," Alice agreed, but she didn't follow Maisie. "It seemed to go all round the room. Like a ghost was flying around us."

"I think it was from the fireplace," Maisie muttered. Digging her nails into her palms, she crept over toward the little grate and

looked at it curiously. It was full of sticks,
as though someone had been trying to light
a fire. "Ghosts don't need fires," she told
herself firmly, and leaned farther in to peer
up the chimney.

Another terrible scream echoed down, and
Maisie screamed back, stumbling and slipping
onto her side. There was a strange chattering
noise and a squawking, and another pile of
sticks and soot fell into the grate.

Maisie stared at it and then wriggled
closer and looked up the chimney again.
Then she coughed as another cloud of soot
collapsed down the chimney and left black
smudges all over her face.

"What is it?" Alice gasped. "Come away
from it, Maisie!"

"It's magpies!" Maisie began to laugh.
"Oh, Alice, that's all it is! A flock of magpies!

I saw them in the big trees on the drive when I went down to the village, and they were screeching like anything, but I never thought about it. They must have made nests on top of the other chimneys too—that's why the fires don't draw properly!" She leaned forward suddenly and dug about among the sticks in the fireplace. "And look! Your bracelet, Alice! And Miss Sidebotham's spectacles. And one, two, three, four silver spoons!"

"How on earth did all that get there?" Alice demanded, running forward. She snatched up her bracelet and slipped it back on to her wrist with a grateful smile.

"Professor Tobin told me a story about a magpie once," Maisie said, running the gold chain through her fingers as she tried to remember. "There was a girl who was accused of stealing, but it turned out it was a magpie all along. They like shiny things and they hide them in their nests." She giggled. "I saw seven of them, I remember now. *Seven for a secret, never to be told.* But we found their secret after all!"

"There's a carriage coming down the drive!" Maisie reported to Alice the next morning as they were playing with the kittens. The bread had looked rather flat and strange after it had been baked, but it had tasted nice and they had made toast for breakfast. Miss Sidebotham complained bitterly that there wasn't anything more substantial, but she still wouldn't even think of descending to the kitchens to help. And she had been grateful for the return of her spectacles, although the first thing she did was to put them on and tell Maisie off for letting the drawing room get so disgracefully dusty.

Alice got up carefully, cradling a white kitten against her shoulder as she came to look out of the bedroom window. "Do you think it's Papa coming to fetch us?" she asked excitedly. "I shall ask if we can take the dear cat and her kittens home with us. We can't possibly leave them here all on their own. I'm going to name the mother Snowflake, but I haven't decided on names for the kittens yet. You'll have to help me, Maisie. We can make a list. It will be a good way to keep ourselves busy on the journey home."

"I don't think Miss Sidebotham likes cats," Maisie warned her, but Alice's eyes flashed.

"I don't care! I shall tell Papa just how useless she has been and how you've had to do all the work. Oh, yes, it was mostly you, Maisie — I only helped a little." She smiled. "I shall put on my best darling daughter face and cough a little and Papa will let me have a hundred cats if I like." Then she sighed. "But I shall miss being here with you, Maisie. It will be terribly boring back in London, even if I've got the kittens to play with."

"I know." Maisie nodded, although the thought of going back to London and seeing Gran and Sally and Professor Tobin was like a warm glow inside her. "Perhaps you could ask for extra French lessons with Madame Lorimer and then we might have more of a chance to talk?"

Alice shook her head firmly. "Oh no. I'm going to ask Papa if you can visit us properly now, without us having to hide from Miss Sidebotham all the time. Although we might have to leave Eddie in the kitchens—I don't think he will ever get on with my darling Snowflake."

They hurried down the stairs to open the front door to Mr. Lacey, each clutching a kitten, with Snowflake and Eddie jumping from step to step, hissing and yapping at each other. Maisie smiled to herself. She had a feeling that Alice was going to get exactly what she wanted. And it really had been the most exciting mystery. She must remember to tell the professor about the magpies, and she was sure that Gran and Sally would be spellbound by the tale of the ghosts that never were . . .

Activities

Test your detective skills and knowledge
with these activities!

Find the answers on pages 156–58!

Book Quiz

Now that you've read the book, have a go at answering the questions below! You may need to look back over the story to help you.

1. What disgusting dish does Alice say she will throw on the fire if she's served it?

2. How does Mary-Ann the maid hide Eddie from the butler?

3. How many dolls are on the mantelpiece in Alice's bedroom?

4. What does Alice's father smoke?

5. What kind of a train do Maisie, Alice, and Miss Sidebotham board to get to the country?

6. What does Miss Sidebotham find is missing at breakfast time?

7. Why does Maisie walk to the village?

8. What do the girls find behind the library bookcase?

9. What does Maisie feed the cat?

10. Who has been stealing the jewelry and other valuable things?

Spot the Differences

Detectives need to be very observant to spot clues. Can you see six differences in the second picture opposite?

Book Ciphers

Some of the things a detective might have to do are to crack a code, to figure out messages sent between criminal gangs, and to help solve a puzzling crime.

Codes work by scrambling messages so they appear to be nonsense to someone stumbling across them. To read a coded message, you need to have the key, which is like a solution.

In *The Case of the Stolen Sixpence,* Maisie and Alice tried making up their own code, using *Oliver Twist* as a key. This is called a book cipher, and the messenger and the recipient each need a copy of the same book, the key, for it to work.

Below is a message written using this book as a key. You can read it like this:

2, 9, 8 = Page 2, line 9, 8th word = treacle

Now try this message:

2, 9, 8 / 16, 19, 1 / 54, 9, 6
87, 17, 4 / 52, 13, 5 / 15, 18, 1!

And here is a longer one:

13, 19, 8 / 111, 2, 5 / 145, 8, 7
4, 1, 3 / 20, 19, 2 / 58, 5, 8
2, 11, 5 / 107, 10, 6

12, 2, 5 / 24, 17, 7 / 144, 13, 4
8, 19, 2 / 57, 4, 5 / 60, 2, 7
135, 11, 2 / 2, 18, 5 / 143, 17, 2!

Now that you've got the hang of it, why not try writing your own cipher and sending messages to your best friend? Just make sure she has the same book as you, and keep it secret!

 *Answers*

Page 150 — Book Quiz:

1. **Calves'-foot jelly.** This yucky-sounding food was made by boiling calves' feet and was thought to be good for invalids in Victorian times.

2. **By hiding him in the laundry basket.** In those days, washing clothes was exhausting. The maids had to boil clothes in a pot, scrub them with such things as milk, chalk or onion juice, and then turn them through a mangle to squeeze out the water.

3. **Three dolls, plus one teddy bear.** Alice's dolls would have been much more delicate than modern toys. They often had wool hair and porcelain faces, so care had to be taken when playing with them.

4. **A pipe.** Victorian gentlemen liked to make a ritual out of smoking tobacco. They wore special velvet jackets and retired to another room after dinner so as not to upset the ladies.

5. **A steam train.** In the cabin, there would have been a fireman shoveling coal into the firebox,

which heated water into steam and turned the engine. Hot, tiring, and very dirty work.

6. **Her pince-nez spectacles.** *Pince-nez* means "nose pincher," and they were a popular style at the time. They even feature in a Sherlock Holmes story, "The Adventure of the Golden Pince-Nez."

7. **To post a letter to Alice's father.** The postal service was reformed during the Victorian times so that people paid in advance to send a letter using the first "Penny Black" stamps, which cost one pence.

8. **A secret passageway and a staircase.** Grand houses often had small servants' staircases running between floors so the owners didn't have to see their servants going about their business!

9. **Kippers.** These are whole smoked herrings, and they were very popular as a breakfast dish until the early twentieth century.

10. **The magpies!** These intelligent birds are related to crows, and there were lots of myths about them in the past, especially because they like to steal things for their nests.

Page 152—Spot the Differences:

Page 154—Book Ciphers:

Message 1: Treacle pudding, not calves'-foot jelly!

Message 2: Next meeting will be at 31 Albion Street.

Bring your kittens and look out for Miss Sidebotham!

Book One

The Case of the Stolen Sixpence

When Maisie rescues an abandoned puppy, he quickly leads her to her first case: George, the butcher's boy, has been sacked for stealing, but Maisie's sure he's innocent. It's time for Maisie to put her detective skills to the test as she follows the trail of the missing money . . .

The Case of the Vanishing Emerald

When star-of-the-stage Lila Massey comes to visit, Maisie senses a mystery. Lila is distraught—her fiancé has given her a priceless emerald necklace, and now it's gone missing. Maisie sets out to investigate, but nothing is what it seems in the theatrical world of make-believe . . .

Book Four

The Case of the Feathered Mask

Professor Tobin has traveled all over the world, and Maisie loves to look at the amazing objects he's collected on his adventures. Now he plans to donate his collection to the British Museum—including a rare and valuable feathered mask. But when a thief breaks in to the boarding house and steals the mask, Maisie realizes she has a new mystery on her hands.

Turn the page for a sneak peek!

Chapter One

"But I don't see why you want to give all these things away, Professor."

Maisie stood in the middle of Professor Tobin's rooms and gazed at the boxes stacked up around her. Wooden packing cases were shedding straw all over the carpet, which Maisie would have to sweep. But she didn't mind—she was very fond of the professor and quite often lingered over the dusting in his rooms so he could tell her stories about his expeditions.

In return, Maisie would tell him all about the latest mysteries she'd solved. Like how she had discovered that the old lady who lived at the end of the road had a secret addiction to toffee bonbons.

"Won't you miss all your things?" Maisie asked. She lifted up a glass case containing tiny stuffed birds perched on a branch and carefully tucked it into one of the boxes. She would miss the amazing objects they were packing away, even if the professor wouldn't. Although it would be nice not to have so many glass cases to polish.

"Oh, of course, of course." Professor Tobin nodded as he patted a wooden carving lovingly. "But I'm running out of room, Maisie. No more wall space." Then he beamed at her. "A museum is the best place for them. Most of the animal specimens will go to the new Natural History Museum, in Kensington, now that it's finally finished. And the masks and carvings to the British Museum. There's to be a Tobin Room," he added, smiling shyly. "Besides, if I give most of my collection to the museum, I shall simply have to go on another expedition and find some more artifacts, won't I?"

"I suppose so," Maisie agreed sadly. She hated the idea of the professor leaving. His last expedition, which he'd returned from several months before, had been all across South America, and he had told her that he'd been away for years.

"I won't be off for a while, Maisie—don't worry. I haven't finished my book yet. And when I do go away, I shall keep my rooms here in your grandmother's house, and you must promise to look after Jasper for me."

Maisie sighed quietly. Jasper was the professor's parrot, and it was one of her jobs to clean his cage and fill his bowls with water and seed. Maisie had always thought that parrots were intelligent, but Jasper most definitely wasn't. He was very handsome, with beautiful bright red feathers, but he was certainly a birdbrain. He had a terrible tendency to sit in his water bowl and tip it over, and then shiver pathetically in the corner of his cage until someone came and dried him. He didn't talk much, either. He would look hopefully at anyone who came into the room, and squawk, "Bikkit?" That was about it, though.

Maisie's gran couldn't stand the parrot, but the professor was her best lodger. His rooms were the most expensive in the boarding house. Plus, he always paid his rent on time. So she pretended not to notice Jasper at all.

"Yes, I'll look after him," Maisie said. She glanced over at the big cage, which hung from a stand by the window—the professor was convinced that Jasper liked to look out. "Oh, he's upside down," she said in surprise, peering at the parrot, who was clinging to the top of his cage with his knobby gray claws.

"Don't tell him! Oh, too late." Professor

Tobin flinched as Jasper panicked, let go, and crashed into his food bowl, spraying sunflower seeds everywhere.

"I'll fetch the broom," Maisie sighed.

While Maisie swept up the mess, she told the professor about her morning's work. She had actually been paid for her detecting, for once—a whole shilling. Mr. Lacey, father of Maisie's best friend, Alice, had employed her to investigate Alice's new governess. Mr. Lacey had wanted to make sure the new governess was nicer than Miss Sidebotham, who had left her post after a disastrous stay in the country with Alice and Maisie.

Maisie had lurked in the hallway, with a duster, to look at the candidates as they came to be interviewed. "Mr. Lacey just wanted to know what I thought about them, you see. He said I've got a good eye," she added proudly. "It wasn't easy, though. I mean, what do I know about governesses? I did tell him not to even think about the one with the fox-fur collar on her coat, because someone who could walk about with a beady-eyed dead fox around her neck all the time absolutely has to be horrible, don't you think?" she asked the professor.

He nodded solemnly. "They'd have to be."

Of course, the job was made more complicated because Maisie was secretly working for Alice at the same time (although Alice was only paying her in toffee). She wanted to be sure that none of the possible new governesses would try to marry her father. Alice had always claimed that Miss Sidebotham was trying to do exactly that.

It was unfortunate that Mr. Lacey was kind, rich, hardworking, and in possession of a most attractive and curly mustache. Maisie had a dreadful feeling that even the most hard-hearted governess would fall in love with him. Maisie had suggested to Alice that perhaps she should go to school instead of having a governess. Not the ordinary school that Maisie had been to before she left to work in Gran's boarding house, of course, but a smart establishment for young ladies. Alice rather liked the idea, but then she had realized she would have to leave her darling white cats behind.

"So Alice said she'd just have to take her chances with a new governess instead, you see. There!" Maisie glared at Jasper as she swept the last of the sunflower seeds into her dustpan. "Don't do it again, you silly creature!"